THE PASTOR'S DAUGHTER

GIDEON O. OJO

THE PASTOR'S
Daughter

GIDEON O. OJO

THE PASTOR'S DAUGHTER

This is a work of fiction. Names, character, places and incidents are either the product of author's imagination or are used fictitiously. Any resemblance to actual persons, living or dead, business establishments, events or location is entirely coincidental

This Book

is a

Special Gift

From

____

To

____

Date

____

Other books by Gideon Ojo

- Faith Capsule
- The Champion in you
- Touched by Love Forever
- 10 Things God Expects from You
- Pathway to Effective Prayer
- Inspiring & Soul Lifting Bible Verses
- God's Promises
(Encouraging Bible Verses)

Transition

Chapter ONE

TRANSITION

'I am blessed
I am smart
I am focused and purpose driven
Everyone that comes into my world is blessed
I can do anything
Nothing is difficult for me
I am fruitful and productive.'

Maria recited her daily confession as she packed her bags. It was just a day to the big day, and she wanted to make sure nothing was forgotten. 'Olivia, I can't believe I won't be seeing you until after three long months. That's like a quarter of the year. I'll really miss you.' Maria said

'I'll miss you too, sister. Soooo much. It is going to feel so empty here without you. Who will I tell all my school secrets to?' Olivia lamented
'Mum of course.'
'I can't tell mum all the gist you know.'
'But you do know mum is always willing to listen, right?'
'Yes, I do, but mum doesn't know the sister's code.'

Maria smiled and hugged her sister 'You'll be done with elementary school and you'll join me soon.'

Maria Eze, the first child of Pastor and Mrs. Eze of Victory Baptist Church was a tall and intelligent girl. She was 13 years old, and her sister, Olivia, was 2 years younger. Maria was going to high school and was going to be attending a boarding school. It was a Catholic school, and she was excited. She had won a scholarship to study at St. Louis Catholic School. Mum and dad had been immensely proud of her. Although, she had struggled with the idea of leaving home for long, but as she prayed, she felt peace. She would miss Olivia and everyone in church. Her best friend, Temi, was going to be attending a day school.

Temi had been her friend since the first day of elementary school. She and Maria were agemates. Maria had found Temi sitting at a corner of the class sobbing, and she had walked up to her.
'Hey, why are you crying?'
'Because I want my mummy.'
'Don't worry, school will be over soon, and your mum will be here to pick you up.'
Temi looked up at Maria with tears in her eyes.
'Thank you. What is your name?'
'My name is Maria Eze. What is yours?'
'I am Temi Ade, but everyone calls me Tope.'

'Okay Tope, let us go eat our lunch.' And from that day the girls had been inseparable. Sometimes, Maria still referred to Tope as a cry baby. When she broke the news of the scholarship to Temi, she was so excited until Maria told her that it was a boarding school.

'Oh! You're going to leave me all alone here and go on to make new friends.'
'I will always come home on holidays and we can write each other letters.'

'Well, I don't know if I'll have another friend like you in college. I am very shy, and I don't think anyone would want to be my friend.'

'Why would you even say that? You are full of life and a lot of people would love to be your friend, Tope.'
'You say so 'cos you are my friend; you are only trying to be nice.'

'I say so because it's the truth.'
'Look at you, you are smart, beautiful and very kind, while I am not so smart, and I have a face full of freckles. I am also short.' Tope lamented.

'Enough Tope, I won't have you speak about my friend in that manner. I've got an amazing friend. You've got dimples and I have always envied them. You've got a great sense of humor, so quit talking like a loser.'

'Yes ma'am,' Tope said and saluted. Both girls laughed.
'Maria!' Mrs. Eze stared hard at her first daughter. 'Yes mum, sorry I was lost in thought.' Maria apologized.

'Daydreamer' Mrs. Eze said. 'How is the packing going?'
'Very well mum. I have a list of all I'll be taking to the dorm. I don't want to forget anything.'

'Good' her mother said. 'Hurry up dinner is ready; your father is downstairs already and you know he hates cold food.'

Mrs. Eze shook her head, she was going to miss her daughter so much. She was such a sweet child. 'Thank you, God, for giving me lovely children.' She muttered under her breath as she went downstairs.

'Yes, mum!' Maria shouted and quickly finished her packing. She was downstairs in a few minutes.

Everyone, including Bisi the house-help, was already at the table. Mum made sure Bisi ate with them. She believed that house helps should be treated as equals.

Bisi had come to work with them when Maria was only a child and now, she was more than a house-help; she was family.

Dad blessed the food and feasting began. This was one of Maria's favorite meal, spaghetti and fish stew. Mum had made this specially for her because she was going away. Her plate was empty in just few minutes.

'Do you want more?' Bisi asked.
'Of course, Maria always wants more spaghetti,' Olivia said

Maria smiles and nods 'I always want more like Oliver Twist.' They all laughed.

'Maria,' Dad said, and Maria knew that the hour had come for final words.
'Yes Dad.'

'You are going to be away for about 3 months, and so far, that is the longest you will be staying away from home. I know that you are a good child and I continually thank God for giving me such lovely children. I want you to continue to exhibit that godliness as you go to live on your own with other children from different parts of the country. The Bible says, 'Evil communication corrupts good manners.' My daughter do not make friends that will mar your future. Remember all that your mother and I have taught you. I know you will come out strong.'

Maria had tears in her eyes by the time her father finished his admonition. She was going to really miss her family. 'Dad, I won't ever let you down and I will miss you guys so much. Olivia, please, take care of Molly.' Molly was Maria's cat, she got it as a gift on her last birthday and she loved the cat dearly. Olivia promised to take good care of the cat.

After dinner, Maria and Olivia talked into the night. Maria promised Olivia that she was going to tell her everything about life in the form. Olivia said she would want to join Maria in her school when it was time for her to go to college. The two sisters did not know when they finally fell asleep in the dead of the night.

College

Chapter TWO

COLLEGE

'New students go this way.' a senior student directed. St. Louis was an all-girls' school. Maria and her mum saw an office with a tag in front that indicated it was the principal's office, so they went in. Maria looked smart in her new school clothe. She had a striped dress on with a beret and new pairs of shoes.

There were some other parents sitting and waiting to see the principal. Maria and her mum joined the queue.

Many of the parents waiting were parents of new students. Maria looked at the faces around, they all looked eager. She smiled to herself, 'I'm sure I also look eager.'

When it was their turn to see the principal, Maria's mum held her hand and they went into the office together.
'Good morning, I am Mrs. Eze and I have come to register my daughter, Maria Eze.'

'Oh! Good morning ma, the famous Eze who got the highest score in the entrance examination. I am Principal Ogaga. Welcome, please sit.'
'Thank you'

The principal was a good-looking woman and Maria was surprised. Weren't principals supposed to look tough and ugly? Oye, a member of the choir usually told horrible stories about his principal, and Maria already had a terrible picture of high school principals.

The principal's hair was nicely done into a ponytail and she looked quite young. Maybe in her late thirties. Maria admired her sense of dressing. She was wearing her trousers with suspenders and had a smart white shirt on.

Principal Ogaga brought out a registration book and attended to Maria's mum while Maria looked around the office. Maria saw an inscription on the wall that caught her attention, it says 'Believe it, speak it and become it.'

Maria decided that she was going to keep speaking her dreams until they became reality.

'Maria! Daydreamer,' her mum said and Principal Ogaga smiled
'Yes, mum.'

'I'll take my leave now. Be a good girl that you've always been. I'll come to check on you from time to time.'
Maria hugged her mum. She felt all alone now as she watched her mum leave her. Principal Ogaga called a senior girl and told the girl to direct Maria to her hall.

'Don't worry. Maria. You are a smart girl, and you will settle in fine. Follow this senior.'

Maria followed like a lamb. The senior girl didn't say a word to her, she just walked in front and came to a stop at one Mary Slessor hall. 'Go in there' was all she said.

Maria went into the hall and found other junior girls crowding a notice board. She went closer, and just then, a hand tapped her shoulder. She turned around and found a chubby girl smiling at her.

'Hi, I am Abby Chukwu, you look lost. The notice board contains the names of new students and their hostel numbers. What is your name? I will look through the board for your name. I hope we are in the same dormitory because I already like you. My instinct tells me you are a nice person and my instincts never lie,' She smiled and winked.
'Maria Eze.' Maria was surprised by the girl's boldness. She looked very jovial and Maria was glad she at least had someone to talk to. Abby pulled her to the board and they both checked for her name.

'Wow! We are roommates. I knew you were destined to be my friend when I saw you at the principal's office with your mum. Come let us find our room. We have been assigned to room 23.'

Maria followed Abby and they both found their room.

'Let us get our luggage from the porters,' Maria said. Maria was excited that she had a new friend. They both arranged their room together. Classes were going to start tomorrow as today was for all the students, new and old, to settle into the new academic session.

When Maria and Abby had settled in, Abby asked Maria to tell her about herself.

'Well, I am from a family of four: father, mother. and a younger sister. Oh! I forgot to mention my beautiful cat, Molly. and my amazing nanny, Miss Bisi. I attended elementary school at Boston, and this is the farthest I have ever been away from home.'

'Wow! You have such a lovely family. I hope you'll introduce them to me when they come on visiting days. I live with my mum here in California and attended elementary school here. My parents are divorced. I usually spend holidays with my dad and his new family in Boston, so I'll come to visit you one day. My mum never really got over the divorce, so she has not remarried. What's that by your pillow?' Abby asked.

'Oh! It's a Bible. Mum gave it to me on my last birthday.'
'So, you read the Bible? I hardly do. I only attend church when I visit my grandmother. She is a strong Christian and she always forces me to attend church.'

'My father is a pastor, and I am a chorister in church. I love going to church and I have a lot of friends in church.'
'Hmmmmm. My mum and dad never go to church, so I grew up not going to church. I love your hair, it's so

black and wavy. You are so beautiful. I wish I wasn't so chubby.'

'You are beautiful too, Abby. I love your bright skin, and your eyes are so beautiful.'

Abby blushed, 'Mum always says that my eyes are my beauty spot.'

The two girls talked and laughed that it was as if they had known each other for a long time. Finally, the bell rang for the girls to assemble for lunch. After lunch, the new friends met with other new girls and they took a tour around the school. When the bell rang for lights out, the girls were exhausted. The first day at school had been a memorable one, and Maria wrote down all that happened in her diary. She wanted to remember this day forever.

Rivalry

Chapter THREE

RIVALRY

'Abby wake up! Or we'll be late and get punished.' Maria pulled the covers off Abby. The bell had rung for all the girls to assemble for morning devotion. 'I hate devotions. Can't they leave those of us who don't like prayers to sleep? Maria can pray my prayers for me.'

Maria laughed, Abby was such a funny girl, and so outspoken. 'Common, Abby gets and let's go.'

Abby got up sluggish and dressed up. They were among the last set of girls to enter the hall for devotion. Sister Adeola was in charge of devotion this morning. She sang Amazing Grace and the whole school joined her. Maria whispered to Abby, 'Oh! What nice voice she's got.' But Abby was not interested in her voice. Sister Adeola talked on 'Honesty'. She told the girls that honesty was the best policy and that no matter what the situation was, they should always speak the truth.

After the devotion, the girls scrabbled to the dining hall to have breakfast. Breakfast lasted for few minutes and then lessons began.

Miss Tega, the English teacher, was a short, nice woman who reminded Maria of her own mother.

'I wish all the teachers can be like Miss Tega,' Abby said, and Maria agreed with her. She made all the girls feel at ease in her class and they all liked her immediately, unlike the history teacher, Mrs. Larry. Mrs. Larry seems to hate all the new girls; she kept shouting at them that they knew nothing.

'Who was Martin Luther King Jr?'
The whole class was quiet. 'You girls should think with your heads. You,' she said, pointing to Maria. 'Tell me who Martin Luther Jr. was.'

'Martin Luther King was a black American peace advocate who fought against racial discrimination in America during the 20th century. He won the noble prize for peace, shortly before he was assassinated in April 1968.'

Mrs. Larry was shocked. 'You're such a smart little girl. What is your name?'
'Maria Eze, ma.' Mrs. Larry acknowledged the introduction with a nod, then continued.

'Next question, who was the first president of America?'
A very skinny girl raised her hand up. 'George Washington in 1781.'
'Clever, what is your name?'
'Dammy King, ma.' Again, the teacher nodded in acknowledgement.

'When was Nelson Mandela born?'
'July 18, 1918,' Maria replied.
'When did he die?'
'December 5, 2013,' Ebun answered.

'Let's see who will get the next question right. Abraham Lincoln was elected president in which year?'
'Elected 1860 and sworn in 1861 ,' Maria said.
'He was assassinated in what year?'

'April 14, 1865,' Ebun said.
'Who was president after George Washington?
'John Adams 1797-1801 ,' Maria said this time.

'Correct. After John Adams, who was the next president?'
'Thomas Jefferson from 1801 to1808,' Ebun said.
Maria shot her hand up ' Not 1808, 1809.'

Mrs. Larry was pleased with both girls. The bell rang and the History class was over. However, an unspoken rivalry had just started between Maria Eze and Dammy King.

'Wow! Not only do I have a beautiful friend, but she is also highly intelligent.' Abby exclaimed. 'I have never been good with dates; how do you keep all those dates in memory? Did you see Ebun's face when you corrected her? Priceless! I can already tell the best students in the class.' She said all these in one breath and Maria smiled. Maria had to learn to keep up with her friend's conversations.

As the two girls were leaving the class for lunch break, Ebun brushed past them, pushing Maria out of the way. There were two other girls with her, and they giggled. Maria quickly grabbed Abby to steady herself, and before she looked up, the girls were gone.

Abby was furious. 'What was that about? So, this skinny girl wants to war, she can bring it on. I am so ready for her. Jealous witch with tiny legs.'
'Quit using derogatory words. Abby. I'm sure it was a mistake,' Maria replied.

'Stop being the Pastor's daughter for one second, I can smell Jealousy from a mile. That girl is bitter and if she repeats this, she'll have me to battle with,' Abby said angrily. 'Let's go for lunch. I'm famished.'

At the dining hall, one of their classmates walked up to them. 'Hi, I'm Ngozi and I admire how you answered questions in class today. Can I join you guys?'

'Yes, please,' Maria said, and the three girls ate lunch together, chattering.
When the bell rang, they all returned to class and the day went on slowly.

Witness

Chapter
FOUR

WITNESS

'Abby, let us join the school choir group,' Maria said after lights out.
'No, I'm not a church girl and I have a terrible voice.'

'So, what group would you join?'
'Maybe press club or cheerleading club.'
'Oh! Okay. Let's hurry up, the English Mistress would soon be in class.'

Just then, Ebun and her friends walked up to them. The class already had a name for Ebun and her friends; the three musketeers. 'Hi class guru, how are you. The tests are fast approaching, and I hope you are very prepared because I am getting ready to watch you come second, while I get the highest in all subjects.'

'Shut up!' Abby said, 'You are such a bitter soul, and trust me, I am going to be laughing my ass out when Maria gets the highest score as she always does.' Abby was so angry.

'Hey Abby, ignore her,' Maria said.
Ebun laughed, 'Hey chubby, the guru doesn't need a bodyguard, so back off. You are not Ngozi Parks, so stop acting like one.' And with that, she and her friends zoomed off.

'Maria you should have left me to handle her, you are too soft, because you a pastor's daughter. I'll give her just a piece of my mind and she'll never recover. Skinny witch.'

'It isn't worth it Abby,' Maria said. 'Let us go'.
'What are you reading?' Abby asked as Maria was so focused on something.

'The Bible. I am reading about Joseph and how God brought him out of the prison to the palace.'
'Tell me about it.'

'Joseph was loved by his father, Jacob, because he, Joseph, was a child Jacob had in his old age. Joseph's brothers were jealous, and they decided to kill him, but Reuben, the eldest brother, pleaded with them not to. He told them to cast him into a pit instead. Reuben's intention was to rescue Joseph after, but when Reuben left, they decided to sell him and lie to their father that a beast had devoured Joseph.

Jacob mourned his son for days. Joseph was sold by the Midianite that bought him to an Egyptian. God was with Joseph and gave him favor with his master. Joseph's master, Potiphar, put him in charge of everything in the house. Joseph was a handsome young man and very soon Potiphar's wife was lusting after him. When he refused to sleep with her, she lied to her husband that Joseph attempted to rape her. Joseph was thrown into prison. There he interpreted people's dream to them.

Pharaoh, the ruler over Egypt, dreamt and no one could interpret the dream. Joseph was then called from prison. He did not only interpret the dream, but he also gave the solution to the problem. Because of this, Pharaoh made him the second in command over Egypt.

'Wow! That is such a touching story,' Abby said
'Well, Abby, I noticed that you rarely attend fellowships. Why?'
'Because I don't think God likes me.'
'Why would you even say that? God loves you.

'No, he doesn't. If he does, my parents wouldn't be divorced. Hurry or we will be late for music class, and Mr. Dele will not be pleased with us,' She said, dismissing the topic.

Maria didn't know what to say, but she did what her mother always advised her to do. She prayed for her friend.

Visiting Day

Chapter FIVE

VISITING DAY

It was the school's visiting day and Maria was so excited. Her mum was coming to see her. She wished Olivia could come too, but Olivia was going to be in school. All the class one girls could hardly sit still in class; they were all eager to see their parents.

'Abby is your mum coming today?'
'She would be coming. I can't wait to meet your mum and introduce you to my mum.'

'I can't wait too.'
The two girls were so excited that they couldn't even pay attention in class.

'Maria, you seem so preoccupied today,' Miss Tega observed.

Abby's mum came first. She looked like a young lady in her twenties, and Maria found it difficult to believe that she had a child as old as Abby. She wore a beautiful gown and looked so full of life. Abby pulled Maria's hand and introduced her to her mum. 'Mum, meet Maria Eze, my best friend and the cleverest girl in my class,'Abby said excitedly.

'Hi Maria, I am glad to meet you. If Abby says you are clever, then you must be really clever….'
Maria smiled. 'Thank you, ma'am, and I am so glad to meet you too. Abby didn't tell me that you are so beautiful.'

'Oh! Thanks, dear. Such a smart little girl.'
Miss Tega, Abby's mum didn't stay too long, she said she had to get back to work. Abby asked Maria what Maria thought of her mum. 'She's very nice and pretty and she looks so young,' Maria recounted.

'I know, everyone says that. She had me when she was 19.'
'Wow! That's pretty young.'
Maria was starting to think that maybe her mother wasn't going to make it again when she showed up.

'Oh! Mom, I thought you weren't going to come again. How are you? How are dad, Olivia, and Molly. How about Aunt Bibi? Did everyone at the church miss me? And how is Tope?
'Easy girl,' her mum said. 'Your dad and Olivia are fine. Bibi is fine too, and Olivia is taking good care of Molly. They all miss you. The church folks can't wait to see you during the holidays. They miss you so much. Tope sends her love; she is doing well in her new school.

'Oh, dear mum. I miss everyone so much,' Maria said. She started telling her mother all that had happened in school. She introduced her friend, Abby, to her mum and told her about Ebun. Her mum smiled and told her to be careful. 'You know all of us at home are praying for you. And hope your friend is a Christian?'
'Unfortunately, mum, she isn't. Her parents are divorced, and she thinks God hates her to have allowed the divorce.'
'Oh! Poor child, we would be praying for her.'
Maria didn't want her mum to go when it was time for her to leave. 'I wish you could stay a little longer'. 'I wish

so too dear, but don't worry, the term would be over soon, and we would have plenty of time together. I love you, dear.'
'Love you too, mum. Bye!'

Abby could not wait for Maria's mum to leave before she started talking. 'Your mum is so lovely. She called me pretty and she smiles so much. I think you take after her in looks but you look so much taller. Your dad must be tall.'
Maria laughed. 'Yes Abby, my dad is tall.'

The two girls kept talking about their families as they went back to the hostel. Abby said she was happy to be in boarding school because her mum went on so many business trips, but she was also sad to leave her mum.

'Sometimes, I think my mum cries and tries to hide it from me. She is so lonely. I am the only one she's got. She once told me that when my dad first threatened to leave her, she begged him to stay. As time went on, she realized that he was abusing her because he felt she couldn't live without him, and that when he said he was leaving she told him never to come back and he never did.'

'Do you hate your dad?' Maria asked innocently.
'No, I don't. I actually wish I do, sometimes, but I don't.

He has another family now; they have a son, and I visit them from time to time. I just want my mum to be happy,' Abby was sobbing and Maria felt really sad.

'My mum is a good woman; she deserves to be happy. She can give up anything to see me happy. I know it must cost her a lot to be here today.'

'Don't worry, Abby, she'll find happiness. I'll pray for your mum.'
'You pray too much,' Abby said, and both girls smiled.

There was a bond. Two girls who grew up in two different worlds coming together to bond so deeply. Maria felt like her friendship with Abby was not ordinary, and Abby felt she had found the sister she never had.

That night, Maria prayed so hard for her friend and her mother. 'Dear God, please help my friend's mum to find love and joy again. Lead Abby and her mum to you. Let her eyes open to your love. I know you love her, make her see this. In Jesus name, amen.' She felt at peace after praying.

Competition

Chapter SIX

COMPETITION

Miss Tega chose Maria to represent the school in an upcoming spelling competition with an all-boys' school.

'I know you can do it, Maria. You are a highly intelligent girl.' Maria confessed to Abby that she is scared of not making the school proud.

'Don't worry girl, you are smart, you'll do well.'
Maria and Abby were relaxing under one of the trees in the school compound when Ebun and her friends came.
'Here's the teacher's pet.'
'What do you want Ebun?' Abby said, looking so fierce.

'I wasn't talking to you, smart mouth,' Ebun replied. 'Maria can speak for herself. I heard you begged Miss Tega to allow you represent the school for the upcoming spelling competition against St. Nicholas' Boys School. Well, I hope you don't ruin the trust the whole school has in you. They would be so disappointed to find out you ain't half as smart as you claim to be.' Her friends laughed.
Maria's face was red, and she was incredibly angry.

'Hey Ebun or whatever you call yourself.' Ebun was shocked, Maria had never ever responded to her taunts and she wasn't expecting her to respond.

'Look here,' Maria continued. 'I don't know what hit you so hard in life and left you bitter, but my dear, I pray you heal. You are such a simpleton, and you have pathetic self-esteem. How come I always thought you were a smart girl? Girl get some joy in your life, then you can appreciate the joy in other people's lives. I'll do well in the competition and even if I don't, I'm not trying to prove any point to you. I am not a loser, so I ain't as bitter as you are. And the next time you think you are hurting me with your words, think again. Now if you'll excuse me, I have more productive things to do with my time, you hateful bitter excuse of a girl. With that, Maria grabbed Abby's hand and stormed away.

For minutes, Ebun stood where Maria had left her, she couldn't believe Maria had just spoken those words to her. When Ebun finally recovered, she went into her hostel and refused to come out the rest of the day.

'OMG! Was that you just now?' Abby couldn't believe it. 'I'll never offend you. Jeez! I don't want to ever receive that kind of tongue-lashing you just gave that miscreant.'
'I was miffed. I spoke harshly to her, but she pushed me.'

'Serves the bitter queen right. She'll think twice next time before she talks rudely to anyone.'

Maria and Abby sat down learning new words together. Abby called out words for Maria to spell and Maria spelled them. When she misspelled, Abby corrected her.

The day of the spelling competition finally came, and Maria was so nervous. The competition was hosted by a neighboring school, St. Nicholas' Boys School. The boys of St. Nicholas were smartly dressed and looked prepared. Maria and the other girl, Mary Tega. took their seats on the platform and soon the competition began. Maria's school had 8 points in the first round, St. Nicholas had 6 points. They went on a short break.

As Maria was talking to Abby, someone walked up to her and tapped her. She turned and found the representative from St. Nicholas. He was a very tall boy and he looked good.

'Hi, I'm Temmy, my friends call me Tayo.
"Hi, I am Maria, and here's my friend, Abby.'
'Hi, Abby,' he said then addressed Maria, 'Well, you are a wiz in spelling.'

Maria smiled, why was she feeling suddenly shy? 'Okay, good luck,' he said and walked over to meet his friends. 'Wow! He's so handsome,' Abby said. Maria eyed her. 'What? I didn't say anything wrong,' Abby responded 'And I didn't say you said anything wrong.'
'But Maria, I think he likes you.'

'Please, Abby, I don't even want to start thinking about boys now. I'm still too young for that.'
'Okay, I heard you.'

The two schools had a draw in the final round and St. Louis was declared the winner because of their initial victory in the first round. Tayo walked up to Maria and congratulated her. He looked like he wanted to say more but didn't know how to say it.
'I hope I'll see you around some other time,' he said.

'Maybe,' Maria replied and wondered why her legs didn't move. Abby came up beside her and pulled her.
'Let's go'. Tayo waved and she waved back at him
'You're blushing,' Abby laughed.

'Don't be silly, I'm not blushing,' she said. Abby just kept laughing. The kind of laughter that got Maria angry. Maria shook her head and watched her.
'Now that you are done laughing, let us go.'
'What age do you think is appropriate for a girl to start having boyfriends?' Abby asked.

Maria said she didn't know. 'I think when you feel mature enough. My mum says that relationships are solely for marriage purposes, so if you know you aren't ready to get married, I don't think you have any business keeping boyfriends.'

'Well, when I'm in my senior year, I'm going to have a boyfriend from St. Nicholas.'
'Okay, then wait until senior year'. Maria said.

Holiday

Chapter SEVEN

HOLIDAY

Maria and her friend couldn't believe that the term had passed so quickly, and the holidays had come.

'I am going to miss you so much. I will call you every day,' Maria said.

'I'll miss you too. I wish we lived in the same city.' Abby looked close to tears.

'Don't worry, the holidays will soon be over, and we will be together again.'

Just then, Maria saw her mother's car drive into the school driveway. 'My mum is here.' She waved to her mum. Her mum stepped out of the car and both girls ran up to hug her.

'How are you girls doing?' Mrs. Eze asked.
'Fine ma'am,' both girls chorused.
As they talked, Abby's mum arrived.
'Mummy! Come, I want you to meet Maria's mum.'
The two women hugged and greeted like they knew each other before.

You look so young. In fact, I thought you were Abby's elder sister,' Mrs. Eze said
Miss Tega laughed and said that was what people always said. The girls hugged each other, and each went with her mum.

Maria had barely entered the car when she started telling her mum all that had happened during the term. She told her mum about Ebun and the spelling competition. Mrs. Eze listened as her daughter chatted. She had missed her so much and was surprised to see how much the girl had grown in just three months. She looked leaner and sounded more mature. She remembered how Maria was born. She had been pregnant with twins and three months into the pregnancy, the doctor had pronounced one dead. They said she would have to get rid of the other living baby as the pregnancy posed a threat to her life. She had refused and her husband had stood by her. They kept praying. The baby did not come until after 11 months. She was such a tiny baby and Mrs. Eze had thought she wouldn't live long but thirteen years after, her baby was growing up to be such a beautiful woman.

'So, mum, I am going to miss Abby this holiday. She is such a funny girl. The girls in my class call her the class clown. She has a very sharp tongue. My Mathematics teacher calls her smart mouth.'
Mrs. Eze smiled as she listened to her daughter's talk about school.

'Abby once said she wished our school were a mixed school, both boys and girls. She said there were a lot of dramas in mixed schools, and sometimes, some girls end up pregnant for their classmates.'

Mrs. Eze laughed. 'Your friend is indeed funny. Come on, girl, we are home.'
Olivia and Molly came running as Abby got out of her mum's car.

'Maria!' Olivia screamed. The two girls hugged for a long time.

'Oh! Olivia, you've grown. You are almost as tall as I am'.

'Molly! I really missed you.'

Everyone was happy, Maria was the happiest. She liked school, but there was nothing like been with your family after so long. She quickly changed her clothes and showered before sitting down to the delicious meal Bibi made for her.

'You've really grown M. You look slightly thinner, though,' Bibi observed.

'That's because they don't feed me with food half as good as yours.'

Everyone laughed.

'Don't worry, you can eat all you want these holidays and even ask for more.' Olivia said

'Stop teasing your sister.' Mum said.

Maria and Olivia had a lot to talk about. They talked late into the night and laughed. It felt like they hadn't seen each other for years. Maria told Olivia all about the dorm, about the mean Ebun, Abby and her smart mouth, and the spelling competition.

'So I met this boy called Tayo at the competition and he was very nice. Abby thinks he is cute.'

'Well....'
'Well what?'
'You said Abby thinks he is cute, what do you think?'
'He does not look bad. Don't look at me funny.'
'Was I?' And Olivia laughed.
The next day, Tope came to see Maria. The two girls were so excited.
'Look at you! You've grown.'
'That's what everyone has been saying since I arrived.'
'But you have. Come right here,' Tope said, jumping on Maria's bed. 'We have got a whole lot to talk about.'

'Yes, but remember today is Friday, our movie night tradition. So, we have to go get popcorn from across the street as there isn't any popcorn in this house, select a movie and talk while we see the movie, as our custom was.'

'Oh dear! I miss movie nights. But I didn't come with any clothes to sleep over, I'll wear yours. Let me call my mum and let her know we will still observe movie night.'
'The first few weeks at the dorm, I thought of movie every Friday.'

The two girls hurried to Wale's Bakery Shop.
'Hi Wale'
'Oh my! Maria is that you? Come give me a hug, child.'

Wale was one of the few old persons that Maria knew to be nice. He had lived in Boston all his life and had run the bakery since his mother died about 20 years ago. He was in his sixties, but he still worked like a man of forty. He didn't like children calling him Mr. Wale. 'Just Wale,' he always said. His wife had died of cancer years ago and his only son was far away in Africa, working as a missionary.

'I have missed your popcorn so much. How are you Wale?'
'I am fine child.'
Wale gave the girls extra popcorn, and they went home happy. The two girls chatted as they watched a movie. They soon fell asleep.

The holidays were going to be over soon. Maria and Abby talked every day on the phone. Both girls had missed each other. They couldn't wait for the new term to begin. Maria decided to go to the town library before school resumption. That used to be one of her favorite sport back home.

She went to the library and the old librarian was surprised to see her.
'I have not seen you here in a long time,' the librarian said.

'Well, I attend a boarding school now. I'm home only on holidays.'
'Oh! That explains it.'

She smiled at the woman and took a seat at her favorite spot. She was reading Sons of Fortune by Jeffrey Archer. She was eager to know if Nat and Fletcher, the twins separated at birth, were going to meet themselves at the end. Her mother had told her that she was a twin, but her twin brother died in the womb. She always wondered how growing up with a twin would have been.
'A penny for your thoughts, miss.'

Maria looked up and found a familiar pair of eyes staring at her. Oh! Tayo from St. Nicholas' Boys school.
'Hi Tayo, what a pleasant surprise.'
'A very pleasant one. I wasn't looking to find you here. How are you?'

Maria couldn't help thinking to herself that he was really a handsome boy as Abby had observed.
Tayo sat beside her and they talked about the book she was reading.

'I read the book months ago. Jeffrey Archer is a fine writer,' Tayo said and Maria agreed.

'Who was your favorite character in the book?' Tayo asked.
'Well, Nathaniel,' Maria shrugged.

'Interesting, that's my favorite character too.' They talked for a while about boarding school and what they loved and hated about school. Tayo was a class ahead of Maria and also a year older. Maria thought he acted and talked older than his age.

'My house is not very far from here,' Tayo said.

'Really? How come I don't know you in this neighborhood?'
'Well, I don't know.'

It was running late, Maria closed her book and told Tayo that she was leaving the library.

'Okay, I'll walk you home, if you don't mind.' She didn't and they both walked down to Maria's house.

'Who was that?' Olivia didn't even wait for Tayo to leave before she started asking questions. 'A friend' Maria said.
'Maria, details please. I know all your friends, remember?'

'That's the Tayo I told you about,' Maria said.
'He's cute.'
Maria didn't reply. She just shrugged.

Unexpected Change

Chapter
EIGHT

UNEXPECTED CHANGE

'I can't believe I already feel exhausted and the term just began. Ahhhh!' Abby banged the table and closed her book.
'Abby, this is a library. Be quiet!' Maria warned.

Just one week into the new term and already the work was overwhelming. Lots of assignments and projects, and Maria couldn't blame Abby for feeling tired already.

'Times like this, I hate school.' Abby said. Maria laughed; Abby was such a drama queen.

'Seriously, reading is no fun at times, I don't know how you sit all day reading, Maria, you must be a witch.'
Ebun and her friends entered the library.

'Who do we have here?' Abby said. 'The three Musketeers.'
'Be nice,' Maria said
Ebun and her friends had stopped being hostile since the beginning of the new term. Although, she still didn't talk to Maria, she also wasn't hurling insults at her at every opportunity; and Maria avoided her like a plague. Maria was shocked when Ebun said 'Hi Maria.'

'Hi Ebun' she replied and looked at Abby, as if waiting for an explanation.
'Well, Olympus has fallen. The almighty Ebun has bowed.'
'Be quiet or she will hear you.'
'And what do I care? She can choke on her greeting. Mad Ebun.'
'You know she hates that name, don't call her that.'

'Oh please! Little saint Maria. I'll call her whatever name I choose to call her. She is evil. She must be plotting some evil, and she's trying to hide it by being friendly. I ain't no fool.'

'Abby! You are so unbelievable. Anyway, we have to finish this assignment, I have rehearsals today.'

Maria and Abby were on their way back to the hostel when they heard a piece of sad news that Mrs. Larry, the History teacher just passed on. The girls were shocked. She taught them History lesson yesterday and had looked healthy.

'She was in our class teaching when she slumped,' one girl said. 'The school ambulance came quickly, but she didn't make it to the hospital.'

Maria trembled. She couldn't believe that it was so easy for people to die. She and Abby walked to the hostel without saying a word to each other, both girls were lost in thoughts.

The news of Mrs. Larry's death spread quickly. There were girls in twos and threes discussing the death. Mrs. Larry had been an unfriendly teacher, sometimes mean, but no one would have wished her dead. She was a strong Catholic and never wore makeup. Her skirts were always long, and the girls had always made fun of her behind her back.

That night, when Maria prayed, she asked God to comfort Mrs. Larry's family. She asked God why young people died but didn't get answers. When she was tired of thinking, she fell asleep.

Sick Leave

Chapter NINE

A SICK LEAVE

Maria stared hard at her friend. 'I think you should visit the school clinic; you've been complaining of weakness for a week now.'

'It's just school stress, I'm sure I'll be fine,' Abby replied.
'I insist, Abby. You don't look fine.'
'Okay I'll go to the school clinic, but I'm sure nothing is wrong with me.'

Maria followed her friend to the school clinic. The nurse told her to go to class, as her friend would need to stay at the clinic for a while. Maria felt so alone in class all day. She overheard Ebun and her friend say, 'Where is her bodyguard?' She ignored them and struggled to keep her mind on the lessons.

During the break, Maria went back to the school clinic, but Abby wasn't there. When she asked the nurse she replied, 'Oh, the junior girl you brought in here? The school called her mum, so she came to take her daughter to the hospital. She has to undergo some tests. She is sick.'

Maria couldn't believe her ears. The day went on agonizingly slow and Maria felt tired. The lessons were boring, and she couldn't concentrate in class. For the first time since she left for the dorm, she hated school and being away from home.

'Maria, I haven't seen Abby all day,' Ayo said. Ayo was Abby and Maria's friend, and she sang in the school choir. Maria always thought that if Abby hadn't come to the dorm, Ayo would have been her best friend.

'Abby is sick, she went to the hospital, but she will be back soon.' Maria felt she was encouraging herself by saying her friend would soon be back but deep down, she was unsettled.

'I am sure it is just the stress of schoolwork; Abby will be fine, and she'll come back to school stronger,' Maria said to herself.

When Maria got to the room, she prayed fervently for her friend. She asked God to heal her and everything should return to normal. Later in the day, Ayo came to call Maria so they would go for rehearsal together. The song they were rehearsing was Kim Walker's Miracles. Maria sang with so much emotion.

Heart Breaking Tidings

Chapter TEN

HEART BREAKING TIDINGS

Three months had passed since Abby was hospitalized and Maria had not seen her. Abby's mum had come to pick up her things, saying 'she'll be out of school for a long time.' She didn't offer any more explanation. Maria was confused. She had never felt so lonely all her life. What was wrong with her friend?

'Maria, there's a call for you.'

Maria hurried to go pick the call, expecting her mum.

'Hello?'
'Hi, Maria. It's me.'

Maria's heart skipped when she heard Abby's voice.
'Abby! Where have you been? When are you coming back? Your mum came to pick your things up, she said you won't be resuming school soon. Are you very sick? Oh! Abby, I have missed you so much.'
'Maria.'

Maria realized that her friend was talking very slowly as if she had great difficulty talking.
'Maria.' She was sobbing, Maria could tell from her shaking voice.

'Abby, stop crying. You'll be fine. I didn't know that you were very sick.' Maria too was already sobbing.
'No, Maria, I won't be fine. The test results are out, and all my symptoms show that I have leukemia.'

'What? Leukemia?' Maria was dazed. For a second, she thought she was going to fall. She quickly moved to the wall and leaned on it. She had only read about leukemia; she had never seen anyone with the terminal illness. Maria remembered a movie she once watched, a little boy with leukemia. His parents spent all their money

trying to save him, but he still died. Maria was afraid. Abby! Abby was too full of life to be so terminally ill.
'Maria are you there?'
'Yes, Abby. Sorry, I was lost in thought. So, what are the doctors doing?'

'Well, the doctors are going to decide whether I need chemotherapy or surgery.'
There was a long pause, each girl seemed to have a lot to say, but could not find the words to express them.

'I'll pray for you, Abby.' Maria couldn't stop the tears that flowed freely down her face.
'Don't cry, Maria, you make me sad when you cry. Tell me about school.'

'School has been so boring without you. Ebun and her friends go around saying I lost the will to live since my bodyguard left. I and Ayo are becoming closer every day, but she just isn't you. The room feels so empty. All the class girls miss you. They keep asking me when the class clown is coming back. I don't know what to tell them.'

'Tell them I'll be back soon.' Abby said slowly. 'It is depressing in here and I can't stop thinking about school. The nurses and doctors are nice, but I have never liked the hospital. Yesterday, my dad and stepmom came to see me. My mum cries every day. She turns down business trips. I overheard her telling my aunt on the phone that if I die, she will kill herself.' Abby sobbed.

'I don't want to die, Maria, I don't want my mum to be alone.'
'Hey! Don't talk about death. You won't die. You'll take the chemo and be fine. You'll come back to school and we will finish writing that story we started.' Maria said confidently.

'I want to believe you, Maria, but I don't know anyone that ever-survived leukemia.'

The bell rung and Maria had to go. She promised to go see Abby in the hospital.

An Unusual Break

Chapter ELEVEN

AN UNUSUAL BREAK

Maria didn't believe the term had ended and Abby didn't return to school. It was months now since her friend had been diagnosed with leukemia. Maria had been praying daily for her. She believed strongly in God's healing power. As Maria sat in the front seat of the car with her mum, she looked lost and confused.

'So, your friend is still sick?' Mrs. Eze knew her daughter well. She could tell Maria was worried. Maria told her about her sick friend when she came visiting. In fact, that was all she talked about.

'Yes, mum. I keep praying, but every time I talk to her, she seems worse.' Maria was crying now. 'Will you drive me to the hospital tomorrow to see her?' She asked.
Mrs. Eze was moved. 'Sure', she said.
'Thanks mum.'

'You know God has all the answers we need. Nothing is impossible for our God. Keep praying dear. Keep praying.'
'Hmmmm' Maria sighed.

Maria was not as excited as she was when she came home the first time on holiday. She greeted everyone with unusual calm. Olivia pulled her in.
'What's wrong, Maria?'
'Abby is sick. Very sick. She has been diagnosed with leukemia.' Maria broke down in tears.

'What? Leukemia? Oh, Maria! That's bad news.' Olivia hugged her sister, 'we will pray, sister. We will pray for your friend.'

That night, before dinner, the Eze family prayed for the little girl battling leukemia. They prayed that God heals her. They prayed like the girl was their own daughter. Maria felt peace as she never felt since her friend took ill.

Maria hated the sickening smell around hospitals. She found Abby lying on the bed but not asleep. She was staring at the ceiling and her gaze shifted as she heard footsteps walk into the room. Her face brightened as she saw her friend.

'Maria!'
'Shhhh! Don't shout.'
Maria looked at her friend long before she hugged her. Abby was a shadow of her former self. The once chubby and vibrant Abby was now a skinny dull-looking girl, lying helplessly on the hospital bed. She tried to sit up and Maria helped her.

'How long do they plan to keep you here, girl? How's the chemo going?'

'Well, I don't know, but I think I'm gonna be staying here for a long time. The chemo isn't really helping. The leukemia wasn't diagnosed on time. I am already losing my hair,' Abby said and took off the head warmer she was wearing. Maria gasped. 'I am so happy to see you. I can't believe I missed the whole term. You will have to tell me what's been happening in school.'

Abby looked so happy, yet she was so sick. 'Maria, don't tell me you are daydreaming again.'

'No, I was just thinking. A lot happened during your absence. A senior girl was suspended for setting her classmate up. She stole some money and kept it in her classmate's bag to implicate her.'

'Wow! Are the three Musketeers still bothering you?' 'They just gossip, but they never come to me.' The two girls were quiet.

'Abby I have really missed you. Every day I go to class wishing for days when we were together. Sometimes, I feel so lonely. I don't even want to be friends with the other girls. Please get well and come back to school. Please, Abby.' Maria wept.

'Don't cry, Maria, I feel so sad when you cry. I don't know if I'll ever get well or if I'll ever go back to school. I don't know. In fact, every day, I don't know if I'll live to see the next day. So I want to just be happy as long as I am alive. I don't want to think about what would happen.' Abby sobbed.

'Don't lose hope, Abby. God can heal you. There's a Bible story about a woman with the issue of blood, she had been sick for years until she met Jesus, and immediately she touched his garment, she was healed. Abby, maybe now is the time to seek Jesus and let Him heal you. I know you have never really believed in him. Please don't accept death. Trust God.'

'Maria, you have been praying, my grandma has been praying. If Jesus was interested in healing me, he would have done so since. He is too busy attending to people who serve him.'

'No, Abby. Jesus loves you and he has time for you,' Maria persuaded.

'Look at this,' Abby pointed to an old Bible lying on the table beside her. 'My grandmother gave me this few weeks ago, but I haven't opened it. I don't think I believe the stories in it.'

The girls chatted for some more minutes before Maria left. Maria wept when she got home. She wept for her friend's lost soul, she wept for her friend's mother that was watching leukemia eat up her lively daughter, she wept for herself, because she couldn't reach her friend.

'Dear God, please do something. I can't find the right words to tell Abby. God, please, don't be quiet.'

immediately she touched his garment, she was healed. Abby, maybe now is the time to seek Jesus and let Him heal you. I know you have never really believed in him. Please don't accept death. Trust God.'

'Maria, you have been praying, my grandma has been praying. If Jesus was interested in healing me, he would have done so since. He is too busy attending to people who serve him.'

'No, Abby. Jesus loves you and he has time for you,' Maria persuaded.

'Look at this,' Abby pointed to an old Bible lying on the table beside her. 'My grandmother gave me this few weeks ago, but I haven't opened it. I don't think I believe the stories in it.'

The girls chatted for some more minutes before Maria left. Maria wept when she got home. She wept for her friend's lost soul, she wept for her friend's mother that was watching leukemia eat up her lively daughter, she wept for herself, because she couldn't reach her friend.

'Dear God, please do something. I can't find the right words to tell Abby. God, please, don't be quiet.'

Infirmity

Chapter
TWELVE

INFIRMITY

The day looked so bright and Abby felt relaxed.

'Morning, Nurse Anu. What time is it?'
'Morning, Abby Binie. It's just 3 minutes past 8am. It's gonna be a sunny day.' Nurse Anu loved to call Abby Binie and she loved the name. The nurse was in her late twenties and she always looked smart. Abby had liked her from the first time they met. Her smile was never out of place, and she was always bringing flowers for

Abby. She dropped the tray she was holding on Abby's table and went out. Abby felt so awake. Her mum would be here soon. As she stretched, her eyes rested on the Bible her grandma had left with her some weeks back. She picked it up and found the story of Sodom and Gomorrah and how God destroyed the whole city with fire.

'And Maria says he is a God of love. How can you destroy people with fire? And you claim to love them.' She flung the Bible angrily across the room. 'Cock and bull story.'

Just then, her grandma walked in.
'Granny Grace!'
'And how's my smart granddaughter doing?'
Her grandma hugged her. As she took her seat, she noticed the Bible in a corner of the room. She looked at her granddaughter questionably before picking up the Bible.
'I'm glad you've been reading this.'

'Well, I just read the story of Sodom and Gomorrah and I can't understand why a loving God will destroy his people with fire.'
Her grandma smiled. 'Child, you have questions, ask God. You are bitter and reading the Bible with

bitterness in your heart won't help. You won't get answers.'

Maria went to the library today, but she couldn't pay attention to what she was reading. She couldn't stop thinking of her friend. Why was her condition not improving? She had been praying or had God stop answering the prayer of his people? She did all that was required of a good Christian, so why was God ignoring her?
'Look who we have here. The genius herself.' Maria looked up to find Tayo standing in front of her. She was in no mood for chit chat.

'Hi Tayo,' she said coldly
'What's wrong? You don't look okay.'
'I am okay. I was already preparing to leave before you walked in.' She said, packing her books. 'Bye!'
'Bye,' Tayo replied looking confused. Had he done something wrong? It was so unlike her to be rude. Maybe something was wrong with her, he thought.

Maria was so angry, but she didn't even know why she was angry. Why were they all asking what was wrong with her? She was okay, but her friend was not. Maria knew that she had been rude to Tayo, who did not even know about Abby's health condition. She thought of going back to apologize but felt she might look foolish.

I just ruined a perfect friendship, she thought as she walked home.

'Hey Maria.'
'Hi Azu,' she wished people would just pass by without greeting, but she had grown up here and a number of people knew that she was the deacon's daughter.
Well, been a pastor's daughter comes with its prize.

'Maria, you have not touched your food, you've been staring at nothing since you sat at this dining table,' Olivia observed.
'Leave me alone, Olivia. I'm not hungry and I'm just thinking.'

Olivia kept looking at her sister as if she was some strange creature. Something was wrong. Maria never snapped.
'Don't burn me with your stare, Olivia, I'll eat.'
'What's wrong Maria? You've been acting so strange lately.'

Maria sighed. 'I don't know why Abby isn't getting any better. I don't know why God won't heal her. I have been praying, but it seems like nothing is happening.'

'Maria, I haven't heard you speak so hopelessly before. Keep praying, she'll be fine.'

'That's what everyone says but she's not fine. She's in pain, she's suffering.'

Olivia didn't know how to console her sister. 'I'm sure all will be well.'

'You don't understand, do you? My best friend is dying and all everyone is saying is that it will be well.' She got up angrily and stormed out.

Olivia was surprised, Maria had never shouted at her before; she had never seen or get her sister this angry. She got up to follow her, but she changed her mind. She would give her some time to cool off. Abby's sickness was tearing her sister apart and she didn't like it. She had been looking forward to the holidays when Maria would come home and they would talk endlessly about everything, but she had been wrong. Since Maria came back, she had been so quiet, talking only when asked questions. She even rarely ate her meals and Olivia knew that it was because her best friend was terminally ill.

'God what's happening to my sister?' Olivia murmured.

After an hour of sitting in the garden, Maria went inside and apologized to her sister.
'I'm sorry I yelled, don't know what came over me.'
'Its fine, Maria. You are under a lot of stress.' The two sisters hugged.

When Mrs. Eze returned from work, only her second daughter came to greet her. She immediately knew something was wrong. 'Where's Maria?'
'She's been in her room all day, not talking to anyone. She hasn't even touched her meal. I think her friend's condition is getting to her.'

Mrs. Eze hurried to her daughter's room. 'Maria, I'm home.' Her daughter was tucked under the blanket, her books were scattered everywhere, and her room looked so untidy. This was so unlike Maria.
'Hi mum' she said without getting up from the bed.
'Maria, look at me.'

Maria got up slowly and faced her mum. Her hair was unkempt. 'Mum, can we talk later, please? My head aches', she pleaded.
'Okay but come have some drugs to cure the headache,' her mum said.

She followed her mother downstairs without saying a word, used the drugs and went back to her room. She refused to have dinner or talk to anyone for the rest of the day. Mrs. Eze was worried, and she informed her husband about Maria's behavior when he got back home.

'I guess our daughter needs our prayer and care,' he said. She nodded.

Mrs. Eze thanked God for the kind of husband she married. He handled everything with wisdom and maturity. When she worried about the children or a member of the church, he always told her that worry solved nothing. She still didn't understand how he lived life without worrying about a single thing.

Dwindling Faith

Chapter THIRTEEN

DWINDLING FAITH

'Where is Maria?' Mr. Eze asked. Everyone was dressed for church, except Maria. Olivia hurried to her room, only to find Maria still sleeping.

'It's Sunday Maria.'
'I know, Olivia. I'm too tired to go to church.'

Olivia was alarmed. They never missed Sunday

services. Never! Even on days when Maria had been sick, she would go, saying that God would heal her if only she could get to church.

Olivia was surprised. 'What is wrong Maria?'
'Nothing, Olivia, leave me please,' she snapped.
Olivia ran downstairs. 'Mum, you won't believe it. Maria is on her bed, she said she's too tired to go to church.'

Mrs. Eze looked at her husband, this was getting out of hand. Their daughter was slipping into isolation and depression. Mr. Eze went upstairs to Maria's room and sat on her bed without saying a word.

'Dad' She broke down in tears. 'I'm sorry, I'll quickly dress up for church now. I'm confused, I don't even know what to believe.'

'You know what, Maria, God never gives us more than we can handle. We will wait for you, hurry and get dressed.'

After the service, Maria didn't greet anyone, she just went straight into the car to wait for her family members. She didn't understand why everyone thought she was acting strange. She just needed space. Even Olivia didn't seem to understand, and it hurts. Didn't they know that her friend was dying?

Some families came over to the Eze's house to have lunch. Maria was so uncomfortable while she sat at the table. These were the same set of families that she was always eager to have lunch with on Sundays. It was a family culture. Members of the church always came over for lunch on Sundays.

'Maria,' Mr. Alfred started. 'I haven't been seeing you in church and you didn't even sing with the choir today. That's so unlike you or have you been spending the holidays indoors?'

Maria looked to her mum and dad for help, but they both shrugged. 'I haven't been feeling too well sir,' she said.
'Oh! You are a busy girl now,' he said, and Maria forced a smile.

When lunch was over, Tope came up to Maria's room to find her sitting and looking so sad.
'Maria, what is wrong?'
'Nothing, Tope, I just want to be left alone.'

Tope left without saying another word. She talked to Olivia about Maria's attitude and Olivia told her what

had been happening.
'I'll pray for her,' Tope said. 'I have never seen her like that.'

Restoration

Chapter
FIFTEEN

RESTORATION

Maria dressed up slowly, she was going to see Abby at the hospital. It was Maria's birthday, but she didn't care. Mum and dad had made her a cake, and everyone had wished her a happy birthday. but she was far from happy. She and Abby had made plans for her birthday. They had planned that Abby would come over and Maria would introduce her to Tope, and the three of them would have a movie night. Unfortunately, Abby was seriously sick. Her life was fading away before her very eyes and Maria could not help her friend.

Abby was asleep when she entered. She went over to Mrs. Folu's bedside to greet her. Mrs. Folu was another terminally ill patient. She had cancer. She was a mother of two boys and her husband, Mr. Folu, came regularly to see her.

During one of Maria's visit to the hospital, Abby had introduced her to Mrs. Folu and Maria had immediately liked the sick woman. She was sweet and always happy, despite her ill health. Maria admired her faith and courage. She had a way of bringing God up in all her discussions.
'Hi Mrs. Folu, how are you today?'
'Hello Maria, I am fine, good to see you,' Mrs. Folu said. On her lap was an open Bible.

Maria was quiet for a while before she asked,'Mrs. Folu, do you believe God can heal you?'
'Of course, I do. I know that when Jesus died, he paid the price for our sins and sicknesses and that this condition is temporal.'
'How can you even have such faith when you are struggling with cancer here?' Maria looked puzzled.

'Maria, you are a smart girl and you have been well trained in the Lord. Do not allow your friend's condition to weaken your faith. No matter our experiences, God is ever faithful. Stand Strong in God's word. I have been praying for Abby and these days, she has been reading the Bible more. Stand strong for her sake. Do not allow the devil to win this battle, for it's the Lord's.'

For the first time in weeks, Maria realized that she was fainting in faith. 'Thank you, Mrs. Folu, you just strengthened my faith.'

Abby stirred and Maria went to meet her. 'Maria is that you?'
'Yes, Abby.'
Abby sat up slowly. She looked so pale and Maria was sore afraid. 'How do you feel?'
'Very weak. Happy birthday, Maria.' Maria was close to tears. So, Abby still remembered her birthday. 'Thank you, Abby, and it is my birthday wish that you recover speedily.'

'Hmmm,' Abby sighed. 'I told mum to bring my diary for me, I want you to have it and keep it. If I don't survive this illness, I want you to keep it.'
'You'll survive, stop talking about death.' The two girls hugged, crying.

Mrs. Folu watched the two girls and smiled. God was sure going to work miracles.

Abby's mum met the two girls chatting. She was happy
to see her daughter looking bright today.
'Hey mum'
'Hi dear and hello Maria.'
'Hello Miss Tega.'
'Is Granny Grace coming mum?'
'She said she would.'
Abby told Maria how her grandma had been telling her
some stories from the Bible and how she was starting to
like the character of Jesus. Maria was glad.

That night, when Maria got home, she apologized to
her parents and her sister for her behavior all week. 'I
don't have an excuse for behaving so badly and I am so
sorry. You guys are the best family anyone could ever
ask for. I think I have been going about with the wrong
mindset. I thought God ought to heal my friend
because I prayed and I have always lived the life of a
saint, but now, I know better. God is God, no matter
our experiences,' she said.

Her parents were so happy. Mr. Eze looked at Mrs. Eze
with a knowing smile. Their daughter didn't know that
they had been praying for her.
'Come here, dear,' her mum said as she hugged her. Her
dad joined and then Olivia.

'Oh, ye of little faith,' Olivia said and both girls laughed. 'I am happy to have my sister back, the Maria that has been living with us these past weeks is not my sister.'

'That faithless Maria is gone.' They both hugged and Maria felt joyful which she hadn't felt in the weeks following her friend's ailment. Now she valued her family more and trusted God, no matter the circumstances. All she was bothered about was getting her friend to see and embrace the love of God. She was going to keep telling Abby about Jesus and his undying love, until Abby's heart opened to the truth.

A Cheerful Spirit

Chapter
FIFTEEN

A CHEERFUL SPIRIT

Maria was on her way to the library when she heard someone whisper her name. She turned and found Tayo standing behind her like a movie star, and studying her intently with eyes like an eagle's. He was wearing a fitted t-shirt that had the inscription 'Truth or Dare,' and the baseball cap he wore was concealing a greater part of his face.

'Hey Tayo, I pick dare,' she smiled, pointing at his shirt. 'Someone is back to her happy self. Okay since you pick dare, I dare you to tell me why you seem so unsettled the last time we met.'

'Hahaha! You're such a smart boy, let us go under that tree.' she pointed to a tree, 'that is where I usually sit when I want to take a break from reading.' Tayo nodded and they both headed for the tree. There was a bench under the tree and some people were around as well. Tayo and Maria settled for a spot.

'Well,' Maria began 'I wasn't exactly in the right frame of mind the last time we met. My best friend is down with leukemia and the doctors are not sure she will survive.'

'Oh! So sorry.'
'Thank you, Tayo. I have been praying but it looks like the more I pray, the worse the condition, so I became angry and frustrated. I think I took my frustration out on you the last time we met. Sorry about that.'

There was a long pause and Maria asked, 'Are you not going to say anything?'
'Well, I am also sorry that you have to go through all these. Sometimes in our lives, we struggle to keep our

faith,' Tayo said and Maria nodded.
'Let's go get some ice-cream,' Tayo said and both of them got up.

'Maria, you know since you won the spelling competition, I have been wondering what kind of person you are. That was the first time your school would win the competition. We have always won.'
'Whoaa! It feels so good to have been the one to break such a big record.' Maria laughed.
'What kind of a girl are you? You are smart and humble, and I really like us to be friends. Just friends.'
'We are friends already, aren't we?'
Tayo nodded.

They returned to the library afterward. Maria didn't read for long as she had to be in church for rehearsals. She waved Tayo goodbye and headed for the church.

Maria was very tired when she got home, she had thought she was going to visit Abby, but of course, that was another day. She fell asleep without taking her meal. In the dead of the night, at about 11:50 pm, Maria woke up. She didn't know what woke her up. Her spirit was troubled, and she had a strong urge to pray. Maria knelt by her bedside and prayed as she had never before. She prayed that Abby would come to the knowledge of the amazing love of God. She prayed fervently, sweating and weeping. She kept praying the Pauline prayers for her friend. She groaned in prayer this way till it was 4 am in the morning, when peace filled her spirit, and she went back to bed.

'Get up, Maria! You sleepy head.' Maria stirred in her sleep. That was Tope's voice, and she knew that Tope was going to keep poking her if she didn't get up. The girl was all shades of trouble.
'Can't a girl rest?' Maria asked and yawned.
'No, it is already past her girl's resting time. I haven't seen you all week and why are you still sleeping? It's 10am.'
'What! I didn't know.' Maria was surprised
'So, thank me for waking you up. What have you been up to?'
'A lot, Tope,' and Maria went on to tell her friend all that had happened lately.

Tope was moved, 'I'll be praying for your friend, Maria.' The two girls had a lot to talk about and Maria moved her visit to the hospital to the next day. It had been a long time since she spent quality time with Tope and she felt guilty. Nothing was going to disrupt movie night today. Maria and Tope talked about everything from books to Bible stories to boys. Maria told Tope about Tayo.

'The most holy Maria is catching feelings.' Tope joked.
'No, I am not catching feelings. Tayo is just a good friend.'

'I am teasing, don't look so serious.'
'Can I join you girls for movie night?' Olivia asked, peeking into Maria's room.
'Sure,' Maria replied.

The three girls picked War room. Although Maria had seen the movie countless times, she was never tired of it. Soon, the room was silent as each girl watched, lost in her own thoughts.

A Painful Gain

Chapter SIXTEEN

A PAINFUL GAIN

'Mum, can you drop me off at the hospital please?'
'Yes, but you would have to dress up very fast. I am running late for an appointment.'
'Okay mum, thank you.'

Maria quickly showered, dressed up and jumped into her mother's car. She had not been to the hospital for days, and she felt a little guilty.

'Mum, how did you feel when you lost your mother?' She asked out of nowhere, as she buckled the seat belt.

'Well, for a while I felt numb. I couldn't believe it. Like you know, I am the first of five children, so I had to be strong for my siblings. I consoled them while they cried and couldn't allow myself to cry. I didn't grieve as I ought to, so the pain of the death stayed for years.' Her mum paused.

'I didn't want to talk about it, I just lived-in denial until gradually, I started to slip into depression. Then, one day, I wrote a letter apologizing to everyone for taking my life and then I took drugs. I was hospitalized for weeks but I didn't die. The nurse that was assigned to me, God bless her soul, helped me face the reality of my mother's death. After then, I started to heal.'

'Hmmm,' Maria said 'that is a touching story. How come you never told me before now, mum?'
'Because you never asked,' her mum said and smiled.

Immediately her mother dropped her at the hospital, Maria ran to her friend's ward. She was incredibly surprised to see Abby standing by another patient's bedside and laughing at a joke.

'Maria, you are here,' Abby said, heading back to her own bed.

'Abby, how are you?'
'Well, I'm not exactly fine. Come, I have a lot to discuss with you.'
'I am all ears,' Maria replied.
'Two nights ago, at about 11:50 pm, I woke up feeling very weak. In fact, I felt like death had finally come, so I just laid on my bed waiting. Then I saw a ray of light coming in through the window. At first, I thought someone was pointing a flashlight in that direction, but as I kept staring, I saw a man clothed in a white garment. Maria, you needed to have seen him. He looked so handsome. I was very afraid. I looked around, but all the other patients were asleep. I sat up slowly in my bed. I wasn't weak anymore, I felt stronger than I have ever felt all my life.'

'The handsome man in white called my name and I was shocked. He urged me not to be afraid that he loves me. By this time, I was crying. He used his palm to wipe my tears and kissed my forehead. I felt so safe with him, I didn't want him to go. He sat there for some time and I fell asleep. When I woke up, he was gone.'

'Wow! Abby you had an encounter with Jesus, the son of God. That same time, I was awake praying for you.

Abby God loves you; I think now is the time for you to accept his love', Maria said.

'I accept,' Abby said to Maria's amazement. Maria led her friend to Christ and told her about the resurrection.

Abby had never felt this joy before. 'Now I am going to rest in Christ, and I know God will take care of my mum.'

As the two girls discussed, Abby's mum came in. Abby told her mum her encounter and her mum too was led to Christ.

Maria felt overwhelmed with joy: this was definitely the best day of her life. Abby's mum soon left the two friends to attend to some pressing office needs. She promised to be back.

'Maria, you have always said that Christians don't die, they only fall asleep. I know I won't survive this ailment, but I know that the devil already lost the battle; what he meant for evil, God meant for good. I want you to continue in faith. You have always been the wiser one of the two of us; knowing the right decisions to make and the right words to speak. I don't want you to give up when I die. I wish I knew this truth earlier but thank God I know the truth now. Never ever allow this zeal for the things of God die. I love you greatly. And please, be a daughter to my mother. You are the sister I never had.' Abby was finding it difficult to talk. Maria was sobbing.

'Please stay, please.'
Abby's mum came back and met the two girls crying. She joined them.

'Mum, I love you,' Abby said weakly. 'Maria, promise me that you would stay strong in faith. Promise me that you will forever share this gospel, promise me that you won't ever doubt the love of God.'

'I promise. I promise,' Maria would promise anything to make her keep talking, to make her stay a little longer.
She smiled 'I see Jesus; he is welcoming me home. Cry no more. Please. I am in good hands.' Abby breathed her last.

Maria felt like someone had just ripped off her soul. She touched her friend for any sign of movement, but there was none. Abby's mum was screaming. The nurses and doctors came in to take the body away.

Maria sat on the bed, quiet for some minutes before she started shaking as she sobbed. The mother and the friend cried with no one to comfort them. The cold hand of death had snatched their loved one. and all they could do was weep for the dead. Maria wept. She wept for her friend, she wept for the promising life death had just cut short, she wept for the star that death had dimmed, she wept for the story that died untold, she wept for the vibrant young girl who was no more.

Moving On

Chapter
SEVENTEEN

MOVING ON

As Maria packed her bags for school, she felt very sad that Abby was never going to come back. She was never going to see her friend again. She looked up at the picture of herself and Abby smiling. Mum had it framed for her and she was very grateful.

'Maria, what are you thinking about?' Olivia said as she entered the room.

'I was just thinking that I would never see Abby again. She was always so cheerful and always had something funny to say. You know Ebun, the class bully? Abby always stood up for me against her.

'Don't worry Maria, with time, the pain would heal.' Maria nodded and continue packing. Olivia helped her and she was done in minutes.

'Welcome back to school Maria. I heard Abby passed on. Sorry dear,' one of the girls at the dorm said.

'Thank you,' Maria wished everyone would stop talking about Abby. Although they all said nice things about Abby, Maria was sick of the constant reminder that her friend was never going to come back.

'They all mean well,' Miss Tega had said. Even Ebun and her friends were nicer to her. They never bullied her again. Abby's death seemed to have affected everyone in different ways.
'Hey Maria.'

'Hi Ayo, what have you been up to?' Ayo and Maria had become awfully close friends.

'Nothing much, I joined the school football team.'
'Wow! Interesting, I didn't know you liked football.'

Ayo smiled, 'I am trying new things this term, I'm living life to the fullest.'

'I love that. Well, I should try something new too, but definitely not football.' Both girls laughed
'Maybe volleyball.'
'Yes!' Abby said excitedly. 'You have got the height.'

'That's the bell for Mathematics. Let's go.'
As days turned into months, Maria learnt to trust God and drop her burdens at His feet.

One day, laying on her bed, reminiscing on the events of the previous months, she had leading to read her Bible. Maria did not have any particular scripture in mind, but she opened it anyway, and found herself staring at the book of Hebrews chapter 4.

Maria read from the beginning, and when she got to verse 9, she paused and read it over again.

“There remaineth a rest for the people of God.”

Maria spent about half an hour thinking about the verse before proceeding to read the remaining verses. The last three verses were the turning point for Maria.

"Seeing then that we have a great high priest, that is passed into the heavens, Jesus the Son of God, let us hold fast our profession.

For we have not an high priest, which cannot be touched with the feeling of our infirmities; but was in all points tempted like as we are, yet without sin.

Let us therefore come boldly unto the throne of grace; that we may obtain mercy and find grace to help in time of need."

It was like light just dawned on her after a long night of pain and sorrow. With each passing day, Maria found strength in God. Prayer became easier and sweeter, and her joy returned. She did not feel too much pain again talking about Abby. Although she never forgot her friend, she moved on, focused on her studies, and became the best student in her class.

Maria had made a promise to Abby that she would be strong in faith and she must keep the promise. She was never late for fellowship and never hesitated to share the gospel with the girls at the dorm. She soon earned the name, St. Maria. She didn't mind being called names, she lived for something and it was to spread the love of God.